A CHILD'S CALENDAR

A
CHILD'S
CALENDAR

Poems by
JOHN UPDIKE

Illustrations by
TRINA SCHART HYMAN

HOLIDAY HOUSE
New York

Text copyright © 1965, 1999 by John Updike
Illustrations copyright © 1999 by Trina Schart Hyman
All Rights Reserved

Printed in the United States of America

A CHILD'S CALENDAR was published first
by Alfred A. Knopf, Inc. in 1965,
with illustrations by Nancy Ekholm Burkert.
The text for this new edition incorporates
a number of changes
by the author.

Library of Congress Cataloging-in-Publication Data
Updike, John.
A child's calendar/by John Updike;
illustrated by Trina Schart Hyman.
p. cm.
Summary: A collection of twelve poems
describing the activities in a child's life and the changes
in the weather as the year moves from January to December.
ISBN 0-8234-1445-0
1. Months—Juvenile poetry. 2. Children's poetry, American.
[1. Months—Poetry. 2. American poetry.]
I. Hyman, Trina Schart, ill. II. Title. PS3571.P4C49
1999 811'.54—dc21   98–46166
CIP   AC

✳

To Liz and Miranda
—J. U.

To Michou and Xavier
—T. S. H.

A CHILD'S CALENDAR

January

The days are short,
   The sun a spark
Hung thin between
   The dark and dark.

Fat snowy footsteps
   Track the floor,
And parkas pile up
   Near the door.

The river is
   A frozen place
Held still beneath
   The trees' black lace.

The sky is low.
   The wind is gray.
The radiator
   Purrs all day.

February

The sun rides higher
    Every trip.
The sidewalk shows.
    Icicles drip.

A snowstorm comes,
    And cars are stuck,
Though road salt flies
    From the old town truck.

The chickadees
    Grow plump on seed
That Mother pours
    Where they can feed,

And snipping, snipping
    Scissors run
To cut out hearts
    For everyone.

March

The sun is nervous
  As a kite
That can't quite keep
  Its own string tight.

Some days are fair,
  And some are raw.
The timid earth
  Decides to thaw.

Shy budlets peep
  From twigs on trees,
And robins join
  The chickadees.

Pale crocuses
  Poke through the ground
Like noses come
  To sniff around.

The mud smells happy
  On our shoes.
We still wear mittens,
  Which we lose.

April

It's spring! Farewell
    To chills and colds!
The blushing, girlish
    World unfolds

Each flower, leaf,
    And blade of turf—
Small love-notes sent
    From air to earth.

The sky's a herd
    Of prancing sheep,
The birds and fields
    Abandon sleep,

And jonquils, tulips,
    Daffodils
Bloom bright upon
    The wide-eyed hills.

All things renew.
    All things begin.
At church, they bring
    The lilies in.

May

Now children may
　Go out of doors,
Without their coats,
　To candy stores.

The apple branches
　And the pear
May float their blossoms
　Through the air,

And Daddy may
　Get out his hoe
To plant tomatoes
　In a row,

And, afterwards,
　May lazily
Look at some baseball
　On TV.

June

The sun is rich
    And gladly pays
In golden hours,
    Silver days,

And long green weeks
    That never end.
School's out. The time
    Is ours to spend.

There's Little League,
    Hopscotch, the creek,
And, after supper,
    Hide-and-seek.

The live-long light
    Is like a dream,
And freckles come
    Like flies to cream.

July

Bang-*bang*! Ka-*boom*!
    We celebrate
Our national
    Independence date,

The Fourth, with
    Firecrackers and
The marching of
    The Legion Band.

America:
    It makes us think
Of hot dogs, fries,
    And Coke to drink.

The shade is hot.
    The little ants
Are busy, but
    Poor Fido pants

And Tabby dozes
    In a pool
Of fur she sheds
    To keep her cool.

August

The sprinkler twirls.
   The summer wanes.
The pavement wears
   Popsicle stains.

The playground grass
   Is worn to dust.
The weary swings
   Creak, creak with rust.

The trees are bored
   With being green.
Some people leave
   The local scene

And go to seaside
   Bungalows
And take off nearly
   All their clothes.

September

The breezes taste
    Of apple peel.
The air is full
    Of smells to feel—

Ripe fruit, old footballs,
    Drying grass,
New books and blackboard
    Chalk in class.

The bee, his hive
    Well-honeyed, hums
While Mother cuts
    Chrysanthemums.

Like plates washed clean
    With suds, the days
Are polished with
    A morning haze.

October

The month is amber,
  Gold, and brown.
Blue ghosts of smoke
  Float through the town,

Great V's of geese
  Honk overhead,
And maples turn
  A fiery red.

Frost bites the lawn.
  The stars are slits
In a black cat's eye
  Before she spits.

At last, small witches,
  Goblins, hags,
And pirates armed
  With paper bags,

Their costumes hinged
  On safety pins,
Go haunt a night
  Of pumpkin grins.

November

The stripped and shapely
   Maple grieves
The loss of her
   Departed leaves.

The ground is hard,
   As hard as stone.
The year is old,
   The birds are flown.

And yet the world,
   Nevertheless,
Displays a certain
   Loveliness—

The beauty of
   The bone. Tall God
Must see our souls
   This way, and nod.

Give thanks: we do,
   Each in his place
Around the table
   During grace.

December

First snow! The flakes,
  So few, so light,
Remake the world
  In solid white.

All bundled up,
  We feel as if
We were fat penguins,
  Warm and stiff.

The toy-packed shops
  Half split their sides,
And Mother brings home
  Things she hides.

Old carols peal.
  The dusk is dense.
There is a mood
  Of sweet suspense.

The shepherds wait,
  The kings, the tree—
All wait for something
  Yet to be,

Some miracle.
  And then it's here,
Wrapped up in hope—
  Another year!

JOHN UPDIKE was born in 1932 in Shillington, Pennsylvania, and studied at Harvard College and the Ruskin School of Drawing and Fine Art in Oxford, England. The author of more than forty books, his works include collections of short stories, poems, and criticism. His novels have won the Pulitzer Prize, the National Book Award, and the National Book Critics Circle Award. He lives in Massachusetts.

TRINA SCHART HYMAN was born in 1939 in Philadelphia, Pennsylvania, and attended the Philadelphia College of Art, the Boston Museum School of Fine Arts, and the School for Applied Art in Stockholm, Sweden. She has illustrated more than one hundred books for children. Her work has received the Caldecott Medal, Caldecott Honor awards, and the Boston Globe-Horn Book Award. She lives in New Hampshire.